*For Bryony and Leonie*

ELMER AND WILBUR

A RED FOX BOOK 978 1 862 30233 4 (from January 2007)
1 862 30233 2

First published in Great Britain by Andersen Press Ltd in 1994
Red Fox edition published 1996
This edition published 2006

1 3 5 7 9 10 8 6 4 2

Copyright © David McKee, 1994

The right of David McKee to be identified as the author of this work
has been asserted in accordance with the Copyright, Designs and Patents Act 1988.

Red Fox Books are published by Random House Children's Books,

61–63 Uxbridge Road, London W5 5SA,
a division of The Random House Group Ltd,

in Australia by Random House Australia (Pty) Ltd,
20 Alfred Street, Milsons Point, Sydney, NSW 2061, Australia,

in New Zealand by Random House New Zealand Ltd,
18 Poland Road, Glenfield, Auckland 10, New Zealand,

and in South Africa by Random House (Pty) Ltd,
Isle of Houghton, Corner Boundary Road & Carse O'Gowrie,
Houghton 2198, South Africa

THE RANDOM HOUSE GROUP Limited Reg. No. 954009

www.kidsatrandomhouse.co.uk

A CIP catalogue record for this book is available from the British Library.

Printed in China

# ELMER AND WILBUR

## David McKee

RED FOX

Elmer, the patchwork elephant, was
waiting for his cousin, Wilbur, who was
coming to visit him.

"He's late," said Elmer. "Perhaps he's
lost. Let's go and look for him."

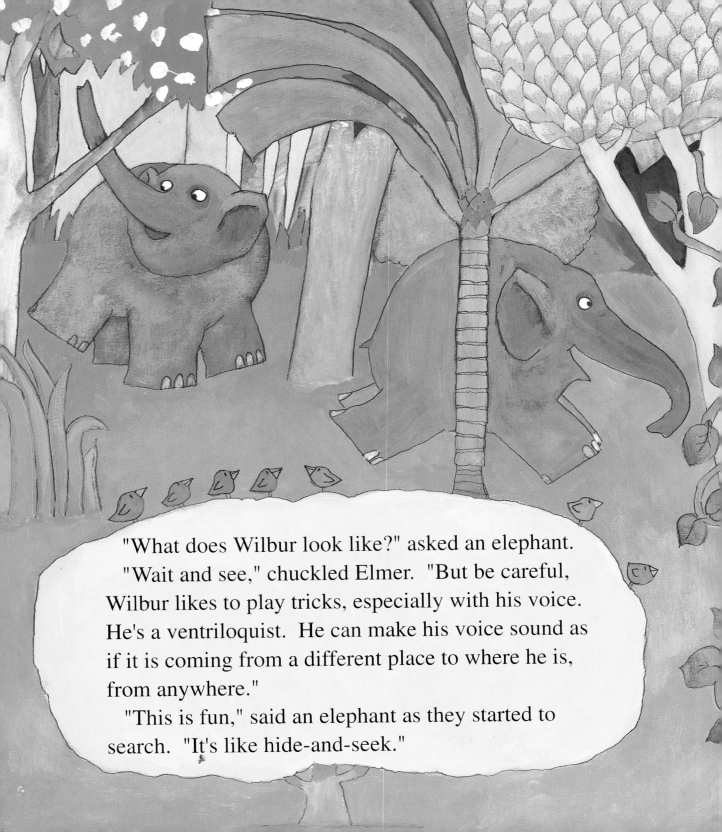

"What does Wilbur look like?" asked an elephant.
"Wait and see," chuckled Elmer. "But be careful,
Wilbur likes to play tricks, especially with his voice.
He's a ventriloquist. He can make his voice sound as
if it is coming from a different place to where he is,
from anywhere."
"This is fun," said an elephant as they started to
search. "It's like hide-and-seek."

Suddenly they heard, "Yo Ho! Elmer! I'm over here."
They rushed to where the voice came from.
"Looking for me?" asked a rather surprised tiger.
"Sorry," said Elmer, "we thought you were my cousin."
"Very funny, Elmer," said the tiger. "Perhaps that's
your cousin I can hear shouting."

"Help!" called the voice. "Help! I've fallen in the pond."

"He has, he has! I can see him!" said an elephant.

"Silly," said Elmer. "That's your own reflection. Keep looking. He's near, but not where his voice is."

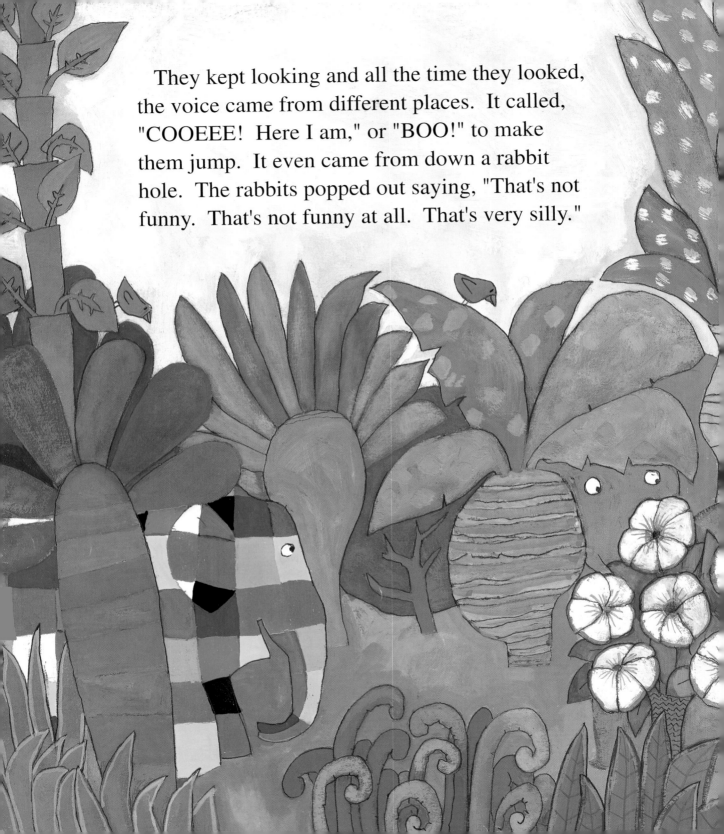

They kept looking and all the time they looked, the voice came from different places. It called, "COOEEE! Here I am," or "BOO!" to make them jump. It even came from down a rabbit hole. The rabbits popped out saying, "That's not funny. That's not funny at all. That's very silly."

After a lot of searching, an elephant said, "We'll never find him, Elmer. Let's give in."

"Wilbur," called Elmer. "We give in. You can come out now."

"I can't. I'm stuck up a tree," Wilbur's voice said from above them. The elephants giggled. "He's very clever," said one.

"If you don't come," said Elmer, "we'll have to go home without you."

"I really am stuck up a tree," said Wilbur's voice. The elephants giggled again.

"Elmer," said an elephant. "Is Wilbur black and white?"

"Yes. Why?" said Elmer.

"I peeped," said the elephant. "He really is stuck up a tree."

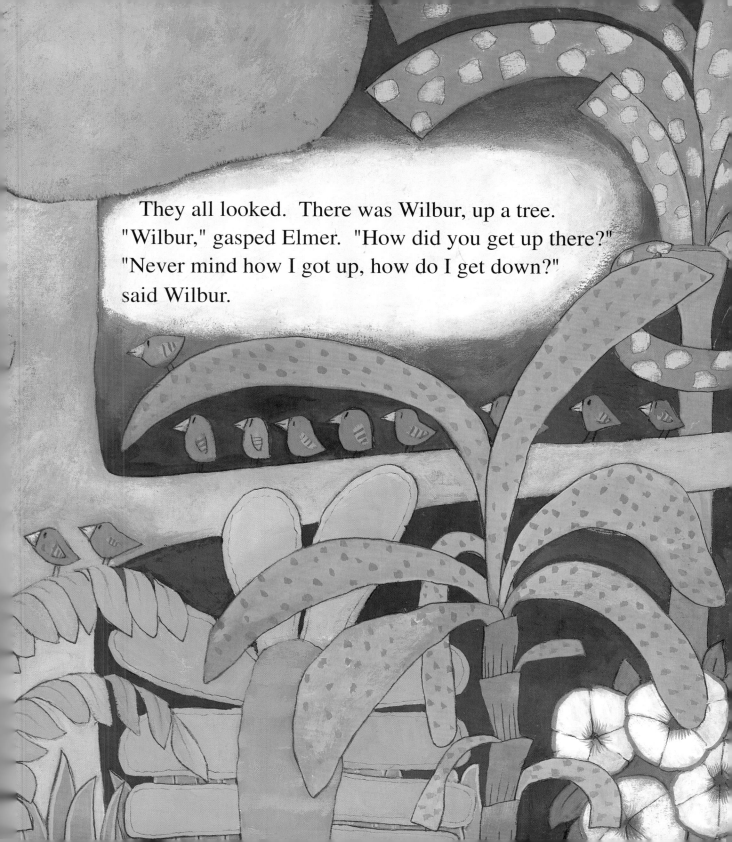

They all looked.  There was Wilbur, up a tree.
"Wilbur," gasped Elmer.  "How did you get up there?"
"Never mind how I got up, how do I get down?"
said Wilbur.

"I've no idea," said Elmer. "But we're hungry so we're going home for tea. At least we know where you are now. Goodbye, Wilbur. See you tomorrow."

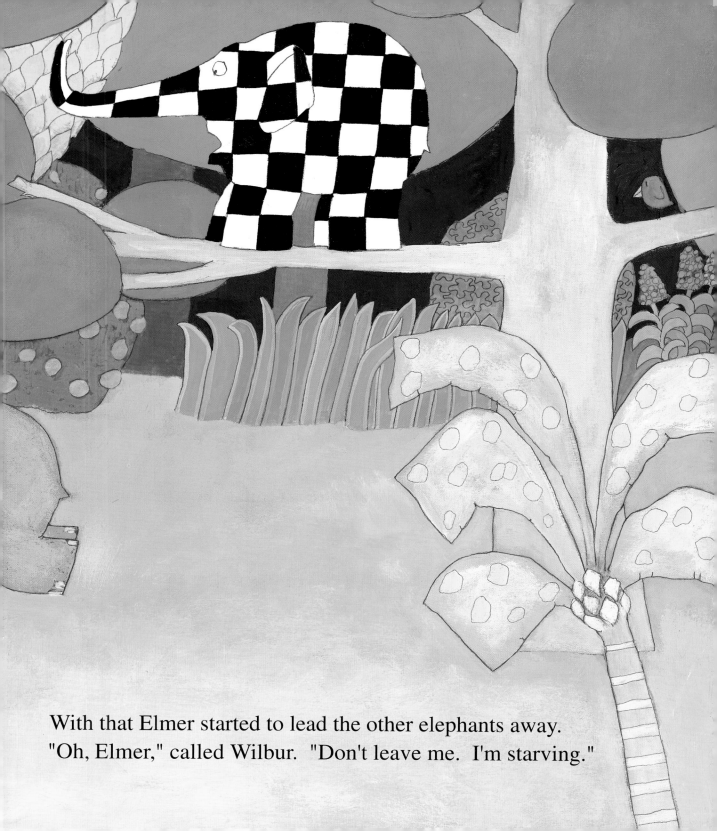

With that Elmer started to lead the other elephants away.
"Oh, Elmer," called Wilbur.  "Don't leave me.  I'm starving."

"Ha, ha, I was just teasing," laughed Elmer, turning back to Wilbur. "If you walk along the branch it will bend down with your weight and we can help you down."

Wilbur walked slowly along the branch. The branch began to bend down. When the elephants could reach, they pulled the branch the rest of the way and helped Wilbur off.

"Thanks," said Wilbur. "Now, where's that tea you were talking about?" Then laughing and joking together they raced all the way home.

That night, as they lay down to sleep, Elmer said, "Goodnight, Wilbur.  Goodnight, Moon."  A voice that seemed to come from the moon said, "Goodnight, elephants.  Sweet dreams."

Elmer smiled and whispered, "Wilbur, how DID you get up that tree?" But Wilbur was already asleep.

# Other Elmer books by David McKee:

**ELMER**
0099697203

**ELMER AGAIN**
0099917203

**ELMER ON STILTS**
0099296713

**ELMER IN THE SNOW**
0099721317

**ELMER AND THE WIND**
0099402637

**ELMER AND THE LOST TEDDY**
0099404168

**MY FIRST ELMER JOKE BOOK**
0099404060

**ELMER'S BATH**
0099503417

**ELMER'S SPLASH**
0099503514

**ELMER IN THE SNOW**
MINI HARDBACK
0862649129

**ELMER AND WILBUR**
MINI HARDBACK
0862649110